GHOST ✦ DETECTORS
Never! Never! Never!

BOOK 9

BY
DOTTI ENDERLE

ILLUSTRATED BY
HOWARD MCWILLIAM

magic wagon

visit us at www.abdopublishing.com

A big thank you to Adrienne Enderle — DE
With thanks to my ever-supportive wife Rebecca — HM

Published by Magic Wagon, a division of the ABDO Group,
8000 West 78th Street, Edina, Minnesota 55439. Copyright
© 2012 by Abdo Consulting Group, Inc. International copyrights
reserved in all countries.

Calico Chapter Books™ is a trademark and logo of Magic Wagon.

Printed in the United States of America
052011
092011
♻ This book contains at least 10% recycled materials.

Text by Dotti Enderle
Illustrations by Howard McWilliam
Edited by Stephanie Hedlund and Rochelle Baltzer
Cover and interior design by Jaime Martens

Library of Congress Cataloging-in-Publication Data

Enderle, Dotti, 1954-
  Never! never! never! / by Dotti Enderle ; illustrated by Howard
McWilliam.
      p. cm. -- (Ghost Detectors ; bk. 9)
  ISBN 978-1-61641-625-6 (alk. paper)
  [1. Ghosts--Fiction. 2. Haunted places--Fiction. 3. Humorous
stories.] I. McWilliam, Howard, 1977- ill. II. Title.
  PZ7.E69645Ne 2011
  [Fic]--dc22
                              2011001841

Contents

The Booger Factory?

"Yay! We're going on a field trip," Dandy cheered as they stood at the bus stop.

"Yeah," Malcolm said. "I hope it's someplace cool this time. That trip to the florist last year was stupid. Who cares about cutting and arranging flowers?"

"Amber Anderson cared," Dandy reminded him. "Remember? She was in the hospital for a week!"

Malcolm remembered. "I wonder why she didn't tell anyone about her allergies."

"I don't know, but she swelled up like a rhino," Dandy said. "And she broke out in prickly hives."

"Yeah, she looked like a cactus with a ponytail," Malcolm added.

Dandy's face lit up as he said, "You won't believe where we're going this year."

Malcolm blinked. "You know already?"

Dandy did a little shuffle. "I overheard some kids talking. Guess where we're going."

Dandy knew something Malcolm didn't? "Where?" Malcolm asked.

"Guess," Dandy said.

"I don't want to guess."

"Come on," Dandy urged, still shuffling his feet.

"Just tell me."

Dandy bounced anxiously. *Bounce bounce bounce.* "Guess."

Malcolm sighed. "Fine. We're going to a piano factory."

Bounce bounce bounce. "Nope."

"A train station."

"Uh-uh." *Bounce bounce bounce.*

"A beauty salon."

Dandy froze and scratched his ear. "Why would they take us to a beauty salon?"

Malcolm snickered. "To get us out of their hair."

Dandy grinned. "Good one."

"So . . . where are we going?" Malcolm asked.

Dandy leaned close like he was afraid someone might overhear. Which seemed silly since they were the only two at the bus stop. "You aren't going to believe it."

"Dandy, just tell me!"

"I heard some kids say that we're going to a booger factory," Dandy whispered.

Malcolm stepped back. "What? There's no such thing as a booger factory."

"There must be," Dandy said, fidgeting with his collar. "That's what they said."

"Maybe they were just teasing you."

He shook his head. "They didn't know I was listening. And they didn't sound like they were teasing."

Malcolm couldn't believe Dandy was serious. "Then they were just making it up."

"But what if it's true?" Dandy asked. "What if we really are going to a booger factory?"

Malcolm thought about it. "What is a booger factory? A giant nose?"

Dandy dug into his. "If it is, I hope it's like a ride where you get in one of those roller-coaster cars and they drive you through. 'Cause walking would be icky."

Were they really having this conversation? "Dandy, we're not going on a field trip to a booger factory. You know why?"

Dandy shook his head.

"Because there is no such thing as a booger factory!"

"I'm only telling you what I heard," Dandy said.

Right then, bus 445 chugged up. Mr. Mullins cranked open the door, and Malcolm and Dandy filed on.

Mrs. Goolsby's class buzzed with chatter about the field trip. Everyone was guessing, but no one seemed to know exactly where they'd end up. Dandy tried to convince a couple of other kids that they were going to a booger factory. No one was buying it.

Mrs. Goolsby entered the room holding a stack of papers. "These are your permission slips for the field trip. Make sure you have a parent sign yours. The field trip is this Friday, so I'll need these back by Thursday."

Everyone waited, but Mrs. Goolsby stayed silent as she passed out the forms. Malcolm was itching to raise his hand and ask, but he didn't want to appear anxious.

Dandy raised his. "Mrs. Goolsby? I heard we're going to a booger factory."

The class burst out laughing.

Mrs. Goolsby stopped in her tracks. "No, Daniel, we're going to the *sugar* factory."

Malcolm slumped back with relief, then turned to Dandy and mouthed, "sugar."

Dandy cupped his hand around his mouth and whispered, "I was close."

Majestic Sugar

Malcolm and Dandy filed off of the bus and stood in line in front of the sugar factory. It was a bright sunny day, but the towering structure blocked out the sun, leaving the class lined up in its shadow.

"How tall do you think it is?" Dandy asked, craning his neck to see the top.

"I don't know," Malcolm answered, "but – *wow!* – it's like a skyscraper!" He had to take a step back to get a peek at the

enormous sign that read:

MAJESTIC SUGAR

Tongue-Tickling Tasty!

There was additional oohing and aahing from the other students.

Mrs. Goolsby walked sharply down the line with her hands behind her back and a whistle dangling from her neck. She looked like a referee just before the big game.

"Listen up!" she barked, staring each student in the eye as she strolled by. "We will behave ourselves, understood?"

The group gave a collective, "Yes, ma'am!"

"No playing or roughhousing, understood?"

"Yes, ma'am!"

"No touching the machinery without permission, understood?"

"Yes, ma'am!"

"No breaking away from the class, or getting out of line. Understood?"

"Yes, ma'am!"

Dandy raised his hand. "Uh, Mrs. Goolsby?"

She nodded permission to speak.

"What if we have to use the restroom?"

"Then you'll do what you just did," she said. "You'll raise your hand."

Dandy twitched his mouth nervously. "But what if the machines are like giants and you can't see us?"

"Then raise your hand and say, 'Mrs. Goolsby, I need to use the restroom.'"

Dandy did another mouth twitch. "What if the machines are so loud you can't hear us?"

A vein on her forehead pulsated. "Then you'll tap me on the shoulder," she said.

Dandy stepped out of line. He tapped her on the shoulder, raised his hand, and said, "I have to use the restroom."

Mrs. Goolsby's vein throbbed again. "Wait till we're inside."

Dandy dropped back in line.

After a moment more, Mrs. Goolsby blew her whistle. *Tweeeeee!* Everyone clapped their hands to their ears. Dandy also crossed his legs.

"Let's go!" Mrs. Goolsby announced, waving them forward. Single file, they marched in through the factory doors.

They were met inside by a woman in a plain blue dress, plastic apron, and what looked like a shower cap on her head.

"Welcome to my little piece of the world!" she singsonged, holding her arms wide open.

Humph. Malcolm whispered to Dandy, "You'd think she owned the place."

"Maybe she does," Dandy whispered back.

Malcolm gave him a look. "Then why is she dressed like one of the school lunch ladies?"

"My name is Lucy Lamont," the woman continued. "I have been a worker here at Majestic Sugar for twenty-five years. I will be your guide for today. You'll be shown a short film, then we'll tour the

refinery. You'll see the tanks, tower, tubs, and filters. You'll learn how sugar beets become sugar crystals. Now, before we start, are there any questions?"

Dandy raised his hand. "Where's the restroom?"

Let's Move On

Lucy Lamont, or Miss Lucy as she liked to be called, ushered them all into a small theater.

"This movie will show you the early beginnings of Majestic Sugar," she explained. "And you'll learn how sugar is refined."

Dandy raised his hand. "No popcorn?"

Mrs. Goolsby glared at him. "This is not the mall cinema. Watch the film!"

The lights dimmed.

Malcolm and Dandy sat through a ridiculous cartoon narrated by Mr. Sweet, the Happy Beet. He looked like a leafy tornado with glasses. And every time a sugar beet was sliced up and added to a machine, Mr. Sweet would say something silly like, "Oh no! That was my cousin, Rollo!" or "I'll miss you, Aunt Pearl!"

Malcolm nudged Dandy. "Are they serious?"

Dandy shrugged.

The movie ended with Mr. Sweet throwing himself into the machine to help make wonderful Majestic sugar for tasty cakes and cookies. Malcolm was a bit traumatized. He decided he'd skip dessert tonight.

"And now," Miss Lucy chimed, "we'll resume our tour." She led them up some very steep stairs to the first vat. It was a machine called a diffuser. A conveyor belt dropped beets into the machine.

Dandy nudged Malcolm. "Think one of those is Mr. Sweet?"

Malcolm smiled. "Maybe his half brother."

"So," Miss Lucy said, "this is the first step to making lots of yummy sugar."

Dandy raised his hand again.

"Yes?" Miss Lucy said.

"Isn't it true that sugar rots your teeth?"

She squirmed a little. "Only if you eat large amounts of it. No one should do that."

"But, to be safe, maybe people should cut out sugar altogether," Dandy added.

"Don't be silly," Miss Lucy squeaked. "Now, let's move on."

She led them up another flight of stairs. "These are the presses," she said.

Dandy raised his hand.

Miss Lucy sighed. "Yes?"

"Isn't it true that sugar makes you fat?"

She gritted her teeth. "Only if you eat large amounts of it, like in ice cream."

"You can't eat large amounts of ice cream," Dandy said. "I tried it once and got brain freeze. My head throbbed for five minutes!"

Miss Lucy roll her eyes before turning back. But just then, the strangest thing

happened. Instead of dropping into the machine, the beets whipped through the air, pounding the students!

"Ooooh! Ouch!"

Malcolm threw his arms up to shield himself, but he still felt the sting of being battered by beets.

"What's going on?" Dandy asked, curling up in a ball.

Malcolm shrugged, letting his guard down. A hefty beet bopped him on the nose.

Kids were swatting and swaying, trying to dodge the flying vegetables. Then suddenly, the beets began dropping back into the presses as usual.

"So sorry!" Miss Lucy said, adjusting her plastic cap. "Let's move on."

Dandy thumped a beet off his shoulder. "What was that all about?"

Malcolm shrugged. "A malfunction?"

Miss Lucy droned on from one vat to another. It all started to look alike to Malcolm. But near the end of the assembly line, one vat stopped completely. They waited a moment, but it was a moment too long. A spout opened and sprayed gooey molasses all over Miss Lucy.

The class let out a collective, "Ewww!"

Miss Lucy wiped molasses out of her eyes, spit some out of her mouth, and said, "Let's continue."

"No wonder she wears all that plastic," Dandy whispered.

Malcolm raised his hand. "Uh . . . Miss Lucy? Does that always happen?"

She forced a smile. "Pay no attention. Sometimes these old machines are fickle."

Finally they neared the end of the tour. Miss Lucy was about to escort them out when a fan revved up and blew her cap right off her head. She snatched it up, crammed it back on, and directed them along.

Near the end of the tour, they came to a padlocked room.

"What's in there?" Malcolm asked.

Miss Lucy put on a fake smile. "Oh, that's nothing. Let's continue this way."

It didn't look like nothing to Malcolm. "Then why is it locked?" he asked.

"It's just a safety precaution," she answered.

Malcolm just couldn't let it go. "What's so dangerous? Is it full of poison? Metal spikes? Wild animals?"

Miss Lucy sighed, shifted her eyes left and right, and in a low voice she said, "I shouldn't be telling you this, but . . . the factory is haunted."

Malcolm should've guessed. Why else would sugar beets fly? "Who's haunting it?"

Miss Lucy bit her lip a little. "You see, there was an accident years ago. This refinery hasn't been the same since."

"What kind of accident?" Malcolm asked.

"A tragic one," she said. She looked away for a moment as though seeing through to the past. "It happened to a worker named Beatrice Salt."

Dandy raised his hand. "There was someone named Salt who worked at a sugar factory?"

"Strange, I know," Miss Lucy said. "But her tale is a sad one."

"Can we hear it?" Malcolm asked. "Please?"

Miss Lucy glanced around again. "You don't mind a ghost story?"

The entire class perked up—even Mrs. Goolsby.

"We can't wait!" Malcolm said.

The Tale of Beatrice Salt

Miss Lucy shook some syrup off her plastic apron and cleared her throat.

"It goes like this," she began. "The factory was built back in 1920, many, many years ago. The owner was a fussy old gentleman named Benjamin Salt. He was bitter and harsh with gray, piercing eyes and a crooked grin.

"Some say that's why he built a sugar factory—to appear much sweeter than he

truly was. But it didn't work. Everyone knew he was a cranky old man.

"He wore the same brown suit every day. He used a spiral wooden cane to hobble from floor to floor. He kept a tight schedule and treated his workers like slaves. When they heard the *tap, tap, tap* of his cane, they stayed busy. No one wanted to be scolded by him. Because when he got angry, it rattled the roof.

"It seemed all he cared about was producing sugar. He wanted Majestic Sugar to be number one in the nation. But there was one thing Benjamin Salt loved more than his factory—his daughter, Beatrice Salt.

"Beatrice worked for her father, typing and answering the phone. She was quite pleasant, and all the workers smiled when

she passed. Some said that she added the sweetness to the sugar.

"But then, Benjamin hired a new worker named Thomas Gale. Thomas was a tall, lanky young fellow who politely doffed his cap every time Beatrice strolled by. They would exchange pleasant words, mostly chatting about the weather or business or if scientists would ever find a cure for hiccups.

"Soon Beatrice was finding more and more excuses to leave the office, just so she could see Thomas. And after a while they fell in love."

Dandy whispered to Malcolm, "Bleh. A love story."

Malcolm shushed him.

Miss Lucy sighed. "This should be where I say 'they lived happily ever after'

and 'the end,' but there was one major glitch. Thomas was just a lowly janitor. His job was to sweep up, empty the trash cans, and scrub all the grinders and tubs. He simply wasn't good enough for the daughter of Benjamin Salt.

"Thomas and Beatrice spent many months secretly exchanging notes and batting their eyes at each other. Then one day, using his broom handle, Thomas

wrote *Will you marry me?* in some spilled sugar. Beatrice used her finger to draw a heart next to his words. They agreed to meet that night at Mammoth Oak, the giant tree by the stream in the park."

Malcolm knew the spot. He and Dandy had waded in that stream a million times.

"But somehow," Miss Lucy went on, "old Benjamin caught wind of their plans. He would never allow his daughter to marry a janitor! He would do everything in his power to keep her away.

"On the day that Beatrice and Thomas had planned to elope, Benjamin called his daughter into that broom closet . . . right there." Miss Lucy pointed to the padlocked door.

"Beatrice stepped in softly, wondering what was up. Why were they meeting in a closet? But the second she entered, Benjamin slipped out and locked the door. 'You'll never marry that penniless peasant!' he shouted. 'Never! Never! Never!'

"Beatrice pounded on the door. 'Let me

out, Father! You can't keep me in here. You can't keep me away from Thomas. We have sworn our love in a heap of sugar. No one can erase that!'"

Malcolm thought maybe they could, but he kept quiet.

"But remember," Miss Lucy reminded them, "old Benjamin was a bitter man. He limped away, leaving her trapped inside. So Beatrice sat, curled up in the closet. With only some bread and water that her father had left her, she was locked in for three whole days."

"Where'd she go to the bathroom?" Dandy mumbled.

Malcolm nudged him. "Shush."

"She tried beating on the door and calling out to the other workers," Miss Lucy said. "But the sound of the machines drowned out her cries. She was left all

alone until the third day when her father unlocked the door and let her out.

"Beatrice pushed passed him, rushing through the factory looking for Thomas. Of course he was nowhere to be found. She ran down to the stream and waited by Mammoth Oak. He wasn't there. She even searched the small, ramshackle hut where he lived. Nothing was there but an old stray cat that had climbed in through the window. Beatrice was heartbroken. Her one true love had vanished.

"She hurried back to the factory to confront her father. He was on the top floor inspecting some beets. 'You!' she shouted. 'You did this!' Then she charged toward him. No one knew what she intended to do. Pound him with her fists? Club him with his own cane? Maybe cram one of those beets down his throat until he choked out an apology?

"No one will ever know. As she stormed toward him, her foot slipped on some molasses and she fell down three flights of stairs. Such a tragedy."

Malcolm imagined poor Beatrice's fall, bouncing like a beach ball down each step.

"But Beatrice never forgave her father," Miss Lucy said. "She's haunted this factory for many years. Now not only does she mess with all the equipment, but in the evenings she roams about, moaning and looking for her true love.

"So you see, Beatrice's story is a sad one, but truthfully," Miss Lucy's eyes darted left and right, "she's one annoying ghost! We've done everything we could think of to get rid of her."

"Like what?" Malcolm asked.

"One of our workers named Bob tried

to trap her in a bottle, but she just picked it up and conked him over the head. Another guy, Arnie, tried spraying her with laundry starch. He figured a stiff ghost would be easy to carry out. Nope. She turned it on him, sprayed him right in the eyes, and fled.

"And Cecil, a packager, tried covering her with the molasses. You can imagine how that went over. You should try dousing molasses on someone who'd skated on it before taking a fatal tumble. It took Cecil two weeks to get all that molasses out of his hair. Nothing seems to work. We've simply given up."

Everyone sat silently for a moment. Then suddenly Miss Lucy went from pouty to perky. She smoothed out her sticky plastic apron and adjusted her cap. "And that's the tour. Here are some sample sugar packets. Thank you for coming."

The Master Plan

The bus was buzzing on the way back. Some kids were creeped out. Some were claiming, "There's no such thing as a ghost."

Malcolm knew better. He nudged Dandy, who was studying his sugar packet like it would be on the next quiz. "We've got some decisions to make," Malcolm said.

Dandy nodded. "Yeah. I know. I'm trying to decide if I want to eat this sugar

straight from the packet or dip my finger in it."

"Not the sugar," Malcolm said. "Beatrice. She's wrecking that factory. She needs to go."

Dandy ripped open the packet, scattering the sugar all over his lap. "Oh no! My sugar!"

"Are you going to help me or not?" Malcolm asked.

"Sure." Dandy tried scooping up the spilled sugar, but it sifted through his fingers.

"Great," Malcolm said.

"But how are we going to get rid of her? There's a bunch of workers there all the time."

Malcolm thought it over. "I think I have a plan."

Dandy licked his finger and ran it over the sprinkled sugar on his jeans. "I'm in."

Malcolm spent a quiet afternoon in his basement lab working out the details. He

pulled out a piece of notebook paper and wrote:

1. *Find a way back to the factory.*

2. *Find a way to convince Miss Lucy to let us back in.*

3. *Find Beatrice Salt.*

4. *Find a way to zap Beatrice Salt without all the workers screaming, running, and fainting.*

5. *Find a way home.*

This would not be an easy task, that's for sure. But he and Dandy had been in worse situations. All he needed to do was find a solution to number one on his list. The rest he could figure out once he got there.

Ew!

Malcolm had his Ecto-Handheld-Automatic-Heat-Sensitive-Laser-Enhanced Specter Detector stashed securely in his backpack. His ghost zapper was wrapped up next to it.

"I've figured out a way to get back to the factory," Malcolm told Dandy. "Just leave it to me."

They padded into the living room where Malcolm's dad sat watching a fishing show on TV.

Malcolm stuck his hands in his pockets and smiled just a little. "Hey, Dad, could you drive us to the sugar factory?"

Dad kept his eyes on the TV. He changed the channel. Some guy with a British accent was making meatballs with an ice cream scoop. "Why? Weren't you there yesterday on a field trip?"

"Yes, sir," Dandy butted in. "But we need to go back."

Dad flipped through two more channels. They flew by too fast for Malcolm to see what was on. "Why?"

"Research," Malcolm blurted.

Dad still hadn't make eye contact. "Research for what?"

Dandy gulped and said, "Mr. Stewart, Malcolm and I teamed up to do a research paper for school."

"And you're researching sugar?" Dad asked.

"No," Malcolm said. "We're researching pests that can get into a factory and spoil production."

"Yep," Dad said, clicking off the TV. "That can be a big problem."

"Bigger than you think," Dandy added.

Malcolm beamed. "And we intend to clean it up."

Dad dropped them off at the front steps of the factory. "Call me when you're done," he said, then he drove away.

Malcolm looked at his watch. "We're too early," he told Dandy. "We need to wait until everyone's leaving."

Dandy fidgeted. "But won't they be locking up then?"

"That's the idea," Malcolm said. "The fewer people the better."

"What will we do until then?" Dandy wanted to know.

Malcolm stepped back and looked up at the Majestic Sugar sign. "Let's scout around, check out the back doors and side windows."

"I don't want to get caught snooping," Dandy said.

"Don't worry," Malcolm assured him. "Just follow me."

They calmly made their way around, walking along the sidewalk that surrounded the factory. There was no sneaking or creeping involved since the side of the building was mostly windows

from the bottom up. It would look awfully suspicious to see two boys hunkered down and tiptoeing to the back.

"Are there any doors here?" Dandy asked.

Malcolm checked out the side of the building. "I don't see any."

Dandy scrunched his face. "But what if there's a fire? What if it consumes the whole factory except this side? What if there's no fire extinguisher handy? What would the workers do? Everyone would be trapped."

Malcolm stopped and faced the dozens of windows on the ground level. "Uh . . . I think they could find a way out."

They strolled a little farther. Malcolm worried that someone would come bursting out of the building and accuse

them of trespassing. After all, he and Dandy were the only people there still in elementary school.

A couple of turns later, they'd made it to the very back.

Dandy held his nose. "It's kinda smelly back here."

It was true. The place smelled like boiled cabbage. "What is that?"

"I don't know," Dandy said, "but it sure stinks."

Seconds later, Malcolm looked up at an open window on the second floor. "Oh no! Look out!"

They'd barely had time to duck when a giant heap of garbage came dropping down and – *splat!* – hit the sidewalk.

"That was close!" Malcolm said, scooting away from the gunk heap.

"Who threw garbage at us?" Dandy fussed.

Right then, two men came bursting out the back door. "Not again," one complained.

The other shook his head. "I'll go get a trash bag." And then he sighed. "I need

a new job. A relaxing job. One with no angry spirits."

"Yep," the other agreed. "We should get paid extra."

Malcolm and Dandy slipped back out of sight.

"Well, that's new," Dandy said. "A garbage-slinging ghost."

"And she was trying to dump it on us!" Malcolm grumbled. "We've got to get in there, Dandy. Now it's personal!"

Ring! Ring!

Malcolm and Dandy backtracked to the front, now worrying about who might see them. It was closing time, so the workers were pouring out the front doors, chattering and saying good-bye.

Then Miss Lucy came out. Her plastic apron was splattered with clumps of sugar and molasses. Bits of her hair stuck out from under the shower cap, like springs boinging from her head. It was obvious .

. . Miss Lucy again had been the victim of ghostly shenanigans.

Malcolm pulled Dandy back. "Wait," he said.

Dandy looked from Malcolm to Miss Lucy then back to Malcolm. He looked like a kindergartner trying to solve a ninth-grade math problem. "Huh? Aren't we going to ask Miss Lucy to let us in?"

Malcolm shook his head. "No, not her."

When the coast was clear, they leaped up the steps. Naturally, the door was locked. But right away, Malcolm could see the person he was waiting for. He tapped on the glass.

A janitor was hurrying long, shoving a broom in front of him. He jumped at the sound of Malcolm rapping on the door.

"We're closed," he called out.

"I know," Malcolm yelled, "but we need to get in."

The janitor shrugged a little. "Sorry."

Malcolm pulled Dandy closer to the door. "Give him your puppy dog face."

"Okay." Dandy tilted his head, poked out his lip, and opened his eyes wide.

The janitor let out a deflating breath and walked over. Dandy's puppy-face worked every time.

The janitor unlocked the door. "What do you need?"

Malcolm could see the guy's name tag— Tim Dugan.

"Mr. Dugan," Malcolm began, "we were here on a field trip and I left something on the fourth floor. Can I go up and get it?"

Mr. Dugan looked up nervously. "You don't want to go up there."

"Yeah, we do," Malcolm said. "It's important."

Dandy nodded. "He's right, sir. It's of the utterly upmostest importance."

Mr. Dugan leaned on his broom and peered over his shoulder. "Can you be in and out in a hurry?"

"Yes!" both boys said at once.

Mr. Dugan stepped back.

"Thank you!" Malcolm called as they ran to the stairs.

"He didn't even ask you what you'd left here," Dandy pointed out.

"I know," Malcolm said, taking the steps two at a time. "And it's a good thing,

'cause I had no idea what I was going to tell him!"

When they reached the top floor, Malcolm unzipped his backpack and removed the specter detector. "Here," he said, handing the ghost zapper over to Dandy.

Dandy held it in the ready position. "Hopefully, this will be fast and easy."

Malcolm gave him a look. "Has it ever been fast and easy?"

Dandy gave Malcolm the puppy face. "Oh . . . right."

"But who knows," Malcolm said, "Beatrice may be our easiest yet."

He'd barely finished the sentence when a nearby phone rang.

"Who do you think is calling?" Dandy asked.

Malcolm looked around. "I don't know. Nobody's here."

Dandy walked over. "It could be for us."

Malcolm rolled his eyes. "No one knows we're up here."

"Mr. Dugan knows."

"Fine." Malcolm snatched up the receiver. "Hello?"

A thin, angry voice warned, "I can't leave. And you can't make me."

"Uh . . . Dandy," Malcolm stuttered. "It's not Mr. Dugan."

Sugar Storm

Malcolm felt a tapping on his shoulder. He slowly turned, facing the ghost. Her faded blue dress hung like a wet towel. And – *huh?* – was that a faded pink rose in her hair or a giant wad of bubble gum?

"You shouldn't be here," she said, floating a foot above the floor. "My father would be angry."

Dandy jerked his head, searching left and right. "Your daddy's still here, too?"

Malcolm held the ghost detector firm and steady. "No, he's not. He's been gone a long time."

Beatrice drifted lazily in front of them. "Not long enough. He locked me in here. I'm trapped."

"Uh, you're a ghost," Malcolm told her. "You can pretty much come and go as you please."

"Oh no," she whimpered, gliding backward. "I'm shut in."

"We know," Dandy said, stepping toward her. "Miss Lucy told us the story."

Beatrice rolled her eyes. "Oh, that blabbermouth? She makes most of it up!"

Malcolm thought of the mess Beatrice had caused during the field trip. And how she'd tried to dump the garbage on

them outside. "Maybe we can help you get out."

Beatrice cocked an eyebrow. "Why would you do that?"

"Because this factory could function much better without all the problems you're causing. Why would you want to wreck the place anyway?"

Her expression went from shy to sly. "Hmmm, let me think. Daddy kept me from my boyfriend, locked me in a closet for days, then caused me to slip on a puddle of molasses and fall down four flights of stairs. Are you kidding? I love wrecking his stinky old factory! And you'll never stop me. Never! Never! Never!"

Beatrice flew high above their heads, then she whipped around a corner and out of sight.

"Where'd she go?" Dandy asked.

They tiptoed forward, peeked around the corner and . . . *Ahhhhhhh!*

Beatrice was waiting for them with a sack of sugar in her hand. She fanned the sack, slinging sugar at them. "Never! Never! Never!" she cried.

The boys blinked and sputtered and spit until the sugar storm stopped.

"Ouch!" Dandy said, rubbing his eyes. "She's not so nice, is she?"

Malcolm didn't answer. He wiped the sugar from his face and shoulders, then took the zapper from Dandy. "She won't get away with this!"

"I think she already has," Dandy said, licking the sugar off his lips. He pointed at the locked door. "She slipped back in there."

Malcolm examined the lock. He pulled, tugged, and yanked. He even tried twisting it. "There's got to be a way into that room."

"We need to do it quick," Dandy reminded him. "Mr. Dugan might come up here looking for us, and then we'll be in a stickier mess than this."

They both laid down flat on their bellies, trying to peek under the crack of the door.

"Can you see anything?" Malcolm asked.

Dandy coughed and sneezed. "Besides dust?"

Malcolm placed the nozzle of the ghost zapper as close to the crack as he could get it. "Maybe it'll work this way."

"You're going to underzap her?"

"I'm going to try," Malcolm said.

He was just about to press the button when – "Ouch!" – he was conked on the head with a sugar beet. *What?* Another came flying and whacked Dandy in the arm. Beatrice had left the closet and was behind them tossing beets again.

"We're being beat with beets!" Dandy cried.

"Okay," Malcolm said. "This lady is really going to get it!"

They threw up their arms, shielding themselves as they charged toward her. She led them around a maze of tubs, tubes, and tumblers. And just as they got close enough to zap her, Dandy tripped over a pipe and toppled to the ground.

"What's going on up there?" It was Mr. Dugan, climbing the stairs.

Malcolm looked around. Beatrice had made her exit—probably back inside the locked closet.

"Nothing," Malcolm said. "We're going."

He helped Dandy up, and they trudged away.

Plan B

"So I guess we go to Plan B now, right?" Dandy asked as they sat outside on the steps of the refinery.

"Yeah," Malcolm answered. "Only, we don't have a Plan B."

Dandy pinched some sugar crystals off his sleeve and dropped them in his mouth. "Then let's think up one. Maybe we could spray her with a fire extinguisher. Once she's covered in foam we could zap her."

"No, it might get into the equipment and damage it," Malcolm said.

Dandy searched for more sugar on his shirt. "Maybe we could bust down that door."

Malcolm shook his head. "She'd just hide somewhere else."

"You're right," Dandy agreed. "We won't be able to get her out."

Then a light went off in Malcolm's head. "No, but I know who can. Hurry, we're heading to the park, and we've got to get there before dark."

Dandy scratched his ear. "What's at the park?"

Malcolm stood and adjusted his backpack. "The Mammoth Oak."

They passed by the swings, the picnic area, and lots of benches. Finally they came to the stream. The Mammoth Oak wasn't hard to find. It towered over most of the park. Malcolm and Dandy had climbed it a dozen times, even though the sign read: *No Climbing!* They were careful to stay away from the branches that stretched over the water.

Malcolm wasted no time juicing up the specter detector. As soon as the power button turned green – *poof!* – a young man appeared before them.

The man sat on the ground, plucking clover and flicking it into the water. He looked wistful and sad. Malcolm might have felt sorry for the guy if he hadn't been wearing such a silly straw hat. It was the kind his dad called a boater. The only other people he'd seen wearing them

were those singers on TV with striped shirts and humongous mustaches.

"Thomas Gale?" Malcolm said, startling the ghost.

Thomas hopped up and faced them. "Yes. Who are you?"

"We're friends of Beatrice," Malcolm fibbed.

Thomas dropped a clump of clover, and held his hands to his heart. "Ah, my sweet Beatrice. How I miss her lovely golden hair, her rosy pink cheeks, and her sweet girlish smile."

"Yeah, well your sweet, rosy girlfriend is a one-woman demolition derby," Malcolm said.

"And you should see her throw a sugar beet," Dandy added. "She could pitch for the Yankees!"

Thomas's eyes beamed. "You've seen my beloved?"

"Yep," Malcolm said. "And we're going to take you to her."

Thomas hung his head. Malcolm could only see the flat top of his boater hat.

"I can't follow you," he told them.

Malcolm squatted a little to see Thomas's face. "Sure you can. It's easy. We lead, you float along behind us."

"No, I mean, I can't go to Beatrice. She doesn't care about me anymore."

"Sure she does," Dandy offered. "Let's go. We've got to get you two crazy lovebirds back together again."

Thomas removed his boater and held it to his chest. His phantom hair was plastered to his head. Who knew that ghosts could get hat head?

"It's useless," Thomas sighed. "If she really loved me she would've met me here that night. She never showed up."

"Look," Malcolm said, losing patience. "She would've if she could've. She didn't meet you here because her daddy locked her up."

Thomas gasped. "Locked her up?"

"Yes! That's what we've been trying to tell you!" Malcolm barked. "Let's go!"

Thomas turned back toward the water. "I can't risk it. If her father finds me there, it'll all be over."

Malcolm deflated. "Her daddy's gone. There's no risk."

Thomas put his boater back on his head and gazed out at the water. "There's always a risk."

Dandy faced Malcolm. "What do we do now?"

"We force him to go."

"And how exactly are we going to do that?" Dandy asked.

Malcolm grinned. "We go to Plan C."

The Dust Scooper

After school the next day, Malcolm opened the door to his mom's utility closet. He pushed aside brooms, mops, and dusters. Then he found it—the Dust Scooper, a handheld vac.

He pressed the button a couple of times, *vrrrrrrrrm, vrrrrrrrrm*, then turned to Dandy. "Let's get him." *Vrrrrrrrrm.*

This time they hitched a ride with Dandy's dad. He was more than happy to drop them off at the park.

"We're going to look kind of silly walking around with a Dust Scooper," Dandy said.

Malcolm hurried past all the kids on swings and seesaws. "Just ignore them."

Dandy rushed to catch up. "Those teeny ones in the sandbox look nervous. Should I tell them the Scooper won't hold that much sand . . . or them?"

"Let's just get to the stream."

When they reached the Mammoth Oak, Malcolm handed the specter detector over to Dandy. "Okay," he said, "we're going to give Thomas one more chance to come peacefully."

Dandy nodded and powered on the specter detector. Within moments Thomas popped into view. He still sat, plucking and flicking clover.

"Is that all you ever do?" Malcolm asked.

"Oh, you again," Thomas said. "No, it's not all I do. Sometimes I toss some acorns in, too."

"There's some rocks over there," Dandy pointed out. "You could try skipping them. That's fun."

Thomas sighed. "I tried once. It was too hard. They just made a small splash and plopped to the bottom. Ghosts can only do so much, you know."

"I don't know," Dandy said. "We're finding out that they can do a whole lot!"

Thomas turned and gazed off past the water. "It doesn't matter. Nothing is any fun without Beatrice."

"Yeah, about that," Malcolm began. "We still think you should go to the factory to see her."

"I told you before, I can't go. Her father won't allow it," Thomas said.

"But she's kinda tearing up the place," Dandy said. "And who knows what she's slipping into the sugar. We have to eat that!"

"Destroying the factory? Good!" Thomas spat. "That factory needs destroying. It would serve her father right!"

"Wow, old Benjamin Salt must've been a real slimeball," Dandy whispered.

"Just come with us," Malcolm urged.

Thomas hung his head. "I can't."

"Then you leave us no choice." Malcolm raised the Dust Scooper. *Vrrrrrrrm.*

And just like in the cartoons, Thomas was sucked into the vacuum . . . feet first.

"Are you sure he'll stay in there?"
Dandy asked. "He's a ghost. He can just
fly out."

Malcolm kept his finger pressed tightly
on the button. "Not as long as the Dust
Scooper is running."

Vrrrrrrrm!

There was probably nothing stranger that day than two boys running along the sidewalk, holding a roaring Dust Scooper like it was a box full of rare baseball cards.

Malcolm held his hand over the nozzle. He worried a little that the battery would fizzle and die, but it *vrrrrrrrmed* with gusto the whole way.

Mr. Dugan drooped when he saw them at the door. "Hey! You boys trashed the place yesterday."

"It wasn't us," Malcolm said over the howl of the vac. "But you know that, don't you?"

Mr. Dugan peered over his shoulder. "Yeah. That's why I do my job quickly and get out." He checked over his shoulders. "She kicked my broom out from under me three times yesterday."

"That's the reason you should let us in," Malcolm urged. "We can stop her."

"No one can stop Beatrice," he said. "She's one hardheaded ghost."

"Please," Malcolm pleaded, "let us in." He didn't know how much longer the battery would last. "I promise we can end this."

"Sorry," Mr. Dugan said. "Go home."

Then Dandy rapped on the glass. "Mr. Dugan, I *really* need to use the restroom."

Mr. Dugan sighed. He sorted through a gazillion keys till he found the one for the front door. "Hurry," he said, then added, "What's with the hand vac?"

Malcolm smiled. "Thought we'd help you clean up."

As soon as they were out of earshot, Malcolm nudged Dandy. "Good thinking!"

Dandy looked surprised. "Huh? I really do need to go."

Malcolm held up the Dust Scooper. "Let's release Thomas first."

They sneaked past the restrooms and up to the fourth floor. Malcolm was sure Mr. Dugan could hear them. But he probably

wouldn't stop them if he thought they could get rid of the factory ghost.

"Hey, Beatrice," Dandy singsonged as they slunk toward the locked room.

Malcolm nodded toward the vacuum. "She can't hear you over the noise."

Right then two sugar beets came flying and whacked them on the back of their heads. Malcolm stumbled and tripped, losing his hold on the Dust Scooper.

It slipped out of his hands and – *blam!* – hit the floor. They waited. After a few silent moments, Thomas drifted out through the nozzle. His boater was ripped to shreds, and his hair stuck out like he'd been caught in a tornado.

Ah-choo! Ah-choo! "Do you know how dirty it is in there?" he said, pointing

toward the hand vac. "It was like a Kansas dust storm!" *Ah-choo!*

Malcolm rubbed his sore head. "Look, I'm sorry, but—"

"Thomas!" Beatrice had sprang up with her hands over her heart.

"Beatrice!" Thomas ran toward her with his arms open. Just as he reached her, she took a step back.

"Ew. You're filthy."

"Thanks to him!" Thomas said, pointing an accusing finger at Malcolm.

"It doesn't matter," Malcolm said. "You two are together again."

"He's right," Beatrice said. "I've missed you so much." She knelt down by a pile of spilled sugar. With her finger, she drew a heart.

Thomas did the same, though afterward the sugar looked sort of brown from all the dust.

"Shall we go away together as we'd planned?" Thomas asked her.

With tears in her eyes, she said, "Yes."

Then she turned to Malcolm and Dandy. "How can I ever thank you?"

Dandy rubbed his head. "You can start by staying away from the beets."

"Yeah," Malcolm agreed. "Just leave the factory and never come back."

"Never! Never! Never!" she promised.

Then Beatrice smiled at Thomas and clutched his hand. Together, they flew up and out of the window.

"Phew! Think they're gone for good?" Dandy asked.

Malcolm picked up the Dust Scooper and held it out.

"I don't know, but if not, we have our handy new tool . . . the Ghost Scooper!"

TOOLS OF THE TRADE: FIVE USES FOR THE GHOST SCOOPER

From Ghost Detectors Malcolm and Dandy

A ghost scooper is a useful tool for a ghost detector. Here are five things you can do with your scooper:

1. Use it to pick up spilled sugar.

2. Run it to get your pet ghost dog excited.

3. Turn it on so the noise covers the sound of your older sister practicing for her talent show.

4. Trap a ghost that is being stubborn in order to make the community a spector-free place.

5. Suck up and transport spirits with it when they refuse to relocate the easy way.
   Warning: Can cause the spirit to become a bit dirty.